Let the Celebrations
B E G I N !

Written by

Margaret Wild

Illustrated by

Julie Vivas

The Bodley Head
London

First published in 1991 by The Bodley Head Children's Books,
an imprint of The Random Century Group Ltd,
20 Vauxhall Bridge Road, London SW1V 2SA

Typeset by Caxtons Pty Ltd, Adelaide
Printed in Hong Kong

First published in Australia in 1991 by Omnibus Books

British Library Cataloguing in Publication Data is available

ISBN 0 370 31605 3

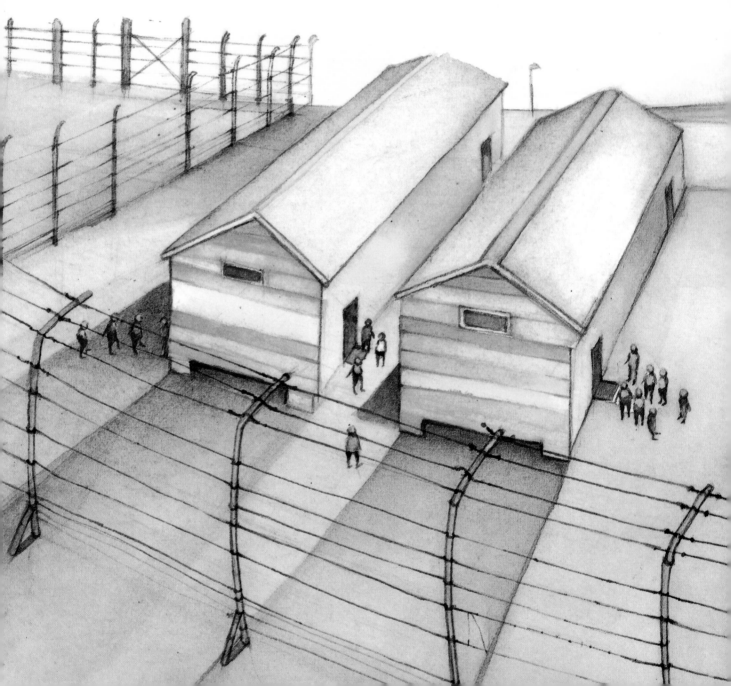

Under Hitler's Nazi regime in Germany (1933–1945) many men, women and children—most especially the Jewish people—were forced into camps, called "concentration" camps. Prisoners didn't have enough clothing or food, and were forced to work very long hours. Millions of these innocent people were put to death during this time—but in 1945, at the end of the Second World War, some thousands were finally released from their imprisonment.

Simple and calm, *Let the Celebrations Begin!* depicts life in a camp and the joy of release and freedom.

A small collection of stuffed toys has been preserved which were made by Polish women in Belsen for the first children's party held after the liberation.

From *Antique Toys and their Background* by Gwen White (B. T. Batsford Ltd, London, 1971).

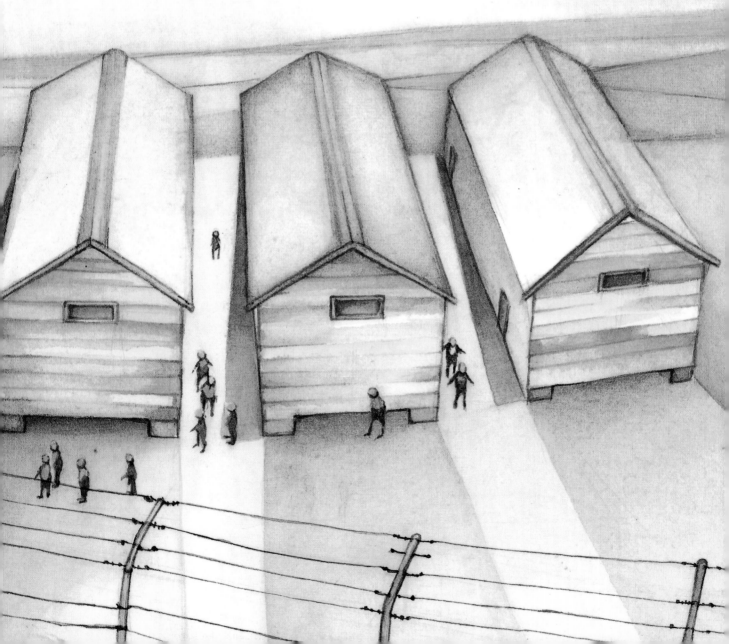

We are planning a party, a very special party, the women and I.

My name is Miriam, and this is where I live. Hut 18, bed 22.

This is my best friend, Sarah, and this is David. He is only four. See him there in the corner with his mama's old black shawl. See his hungry eyes and his legs. His legs! The chickens running in our yard were fatter.

Chickens! It is years since I chewed on a chicken leg.
Back then, I didn't like the skin or fat. Now I would
gobble it all up—skin, fat and bones. I would lick the
plate and pull the wishbone and make sure David had
second helpings, third helpings, fourth helpings
of everything!

Sarah and David think they have always lived here. They think this is their home. But I still remember. I remember Mama and Papa and my very own bedroom and my very own bed and, in the corner, my very own toys.

But we laugh at her, the women and I. And we go on begging buttons and torn pockets, because there is nothing we can do about the food. There *is* no food. But we can make toys. And we shall. In the end, old Jacoba gives us the back of her jumper and goes off grumbling that it will be our fault if she gets rheumatism in her back this winter.

But we shrug and smile because we know we won't still be in the camp this winter. The soldiers are coming soon— everyone says so!—and we must be ready, the women and I, for our party, our very special party.

We are cutting and sewing, all of us, every night while the
guards sleep. Even old Jacoba is helping. She has given us
the right sleeve of her jumper, and she says it will be our
fault—oh yes!—if she gets rheumatism in her right arm
this winter.

But still we don't have enough material! So now we are cutting up our own clothes. My skirt is getting shorter and shorter. David is puzzled. He thinks my legs are growing longer and longer, remarkably fast.

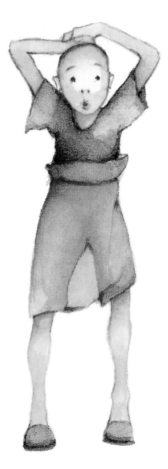

They are here! Everyone, everyone, the soldiers are here!
See their guns and their tanks and the big gates
swinging open!

That night at our party, our very special party, the women and I bring out the toys.

David wraps up his precious owl in his mama's old black shawl.

Sarah hugs her funny patchwork elephant and vows to keep it always on her windowsill.

And old Jacoba tells everyone, very loudly, that she donated her whole jumper—yes!—the back of it, the front, and both sleeves, so that these dear children could have toys.

The women and I wink at one another and pass old Jacoba another helping of chicken soup—

and so the celebrations begin!

Suddenly . . . we heard the sound of rolling tanks. We were convinced that the Germans were about to blow up the camp. But then . . . we heard a loud voice say in German: "Hello, hello, you are free! We are British soldiers, and we came to liberate you!"

We ran out of the barracks and saw . . . a British army car with a loudspeaker on top going through the camp and repeating the same message over and over again. Within minutes, hundreds of women stopped the car, screaming, laughing, and crying, and the British soldier was crying with us.

Recollection of Dr Hadassah Rosensaft, from *The Liberation of the Nazi Concentration Camps 1945: Eyewitness Accounts of the Liberators*, edited by Brewster Chamberlin and Marcia Feldman (United States Holocaust Memorial Council, Washington, DC, 1987).